Easter Elf

Rochelle Groskreutz

Illustrated by Leah DiPasquale

KWiL Publishing

To Ava, Sadie, Clarice, and Rich for your support and inspiration. And to the rest of the "village"
who made this all possible—you know who you are, so imagine me hugging you . . . now :).
—R.G.

KWiL Publishing, LLC
Milwaukee, Wisconsin, USA
kwilpublishing.com

Text Copyright © 2019 Rochelle Groskreutz
Illustrations Copyright © 2019 Leah DiPasquale

Publisher's Cataloging-in-Publication Data

Names: Groskreutz, Rochelle, author. | DiPasquale, Leah, illustrator.
Title: Easter elf / Rochelle Groskreutz; illustrated by Leah DiPasquale.
Description: Milwaukee, WI: KWiL Publishing, 2019.
Identifiers: ISBN 978-0-9991437-7-3 | LCCN 2018953625
Summary: Easter Elf and Christmas Elf partake in friendly competition after
Christmas Elf's reindeer make a crash landing at Easter Elf Spring Training.
Subjects: LCSH Elves—Juvenile fiction. | Friendship—Juvenile fiction |
Easter—Juvenile fiction. | Christmas—Juvenile fiction. | BISAC JUVENILE FICTION /
Social Themes / Friendship | JUVENILE FICTION / Holidays & Celebrations /
Easter & Lent | JUVENILE FICTION / Holidays & Celebrations / Christmas & Advent
Classification: LCC PZ7.G8983 Ea 2019| DDC [E]—dc23

Text set in Esta. Display type is Chunk Five.
The illustrations were created digitally in Adobe Photoshop.
Book design by Leah DiPasquale.

Printed in Stevens Point, Wisconsin, USA.

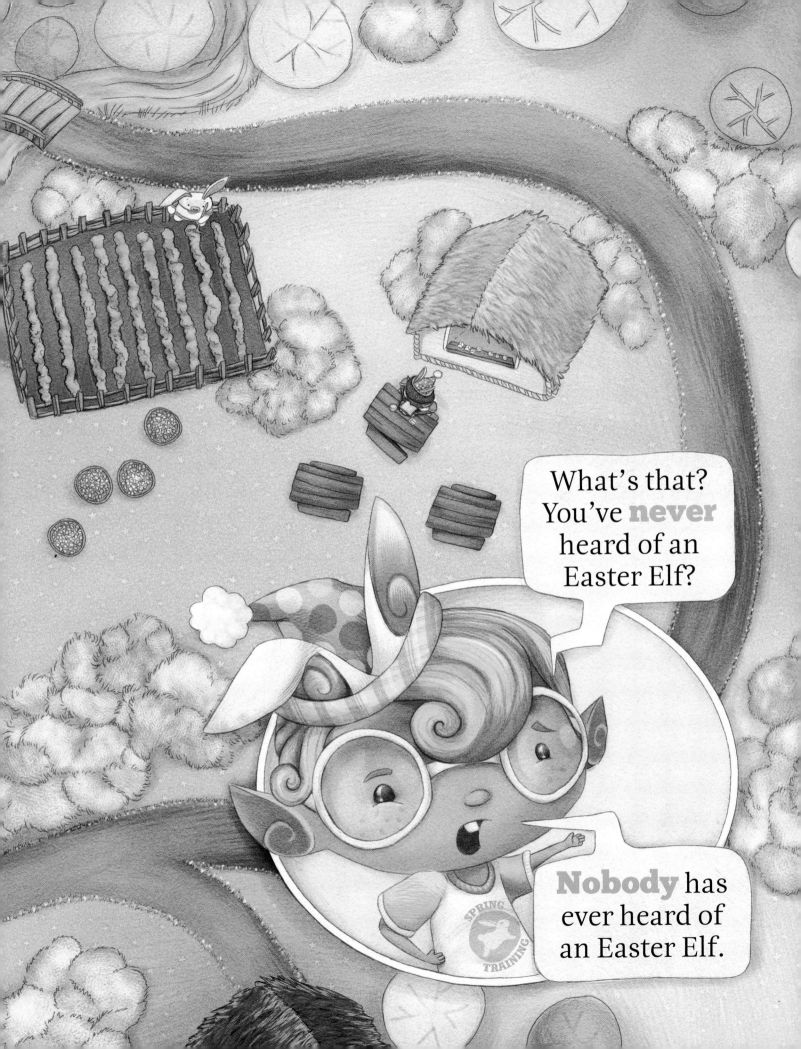

Santa's elves get **all** the glory.

Sure, they make tons of toys,

help train reindeer,

and check the naughty and nice list.

Good for them!

But they wouldn't last one season as an Easter Elf.

We're **egg**ceptional at

basket weaving,

grass shredding,

egg hiding,
and of course, . . .

hopping!

Even **SANTA** hasn't heard of an Easter Elf?

NOBODY has **EVER** heard of an Easter Elf!

Santa, your reindeer-in-training **CRASHED!** Christmas Elf is **HERE**, at Easter Elf Spring Training. Apparently, she gets **REALLY** grossed out by **EGGS!**

OH DEAR! Check the sleigh for a candy ca—

For a what?! Hello? **HELLO?**